# Macy W

By Matthew Lee

BunnyLovesBigCarrots@gmail.com

In the huge mirror, I watched Macy turn her young body first to the left, then to the right, then rising on her tippy-toes. Her brow furrowed.

"I look cheap," she stated. "White trailer-trash."

My eyes wandered from her gorgeous face to her big hazel eyes and full lips, down her throat and large firm breasts, across the ridiculous tight white, V-neck T-shirt her boss was making her wear. The word "*ENJOY*" stretched across her chest in bright pink, obnoxious glittering letters. She pulled up on the V, trying to hide some of the obscene display of cleavage the too-small shirt was creating. She turned her hips to look at her ass in the full-length mirror and a frustrated sigh escaped her lips. The white shorts barely covered more than half her butt-cheeks. She tugged at the legs of the shorts trying to cover more of her.

"I look like a slut," she whined. Some of the other girls turned to look at her. If they had a problem with this year's uniform, I couldn't see it on their faces. In fact, everywhere I looked I saw hot young girls with fantastic tits and ass reveling in their own beauty. Macy's boss Shane was a genius.

"Baby-girl," I began, lowering my voice so the other girls didn't hear. "First off, you are the hottest girl here by far, and there are a lot of hot girls here. Secondly, with your high-cheek bones, big hazel eyes and long dark hair, you couldn't look slutty if you tried to. It would be like Kate Beckinsale trying to look slutty; just doesn't happen. Third, you only have to wear that outfit for three days and your boss will pay you a

1

ton of money, which will make you very happy once this is behind you."

Macy looked at me with faux indignation. "So you are telling me to do it for the money? You're my pimp now?"

I didn't take the bait.

"I'm suggesting you relax and have some fun. Nobody knows us in this city. Soon enough we'll be back to our apartment and you'll be well on your way to forgetting all about how you feel right now. Go take your place at the booth, flirt with the business men, sell a ton of that energy drink, join me at the pool when you're off work, and let's turn this into a fun trip. You look fucking hot in that uniform."

Macy sometimes works these conventions in addition to her regular job. My job allows me lots of flexibility so I almost always travel with her. The money is amazing and we get to visit new cities all over the US.

Her smile had spread the more I talked so by now it was from ear to ear.

"You want me to flirt with the men?" she teased. Leave it to Macy to pick out that one thing. A giant fist squeezed my guts.

Not long ago Macy and I found ourselves in an incredibly awkward and difficult situation at work. We worked together and were secretly dating and due to other circumstances it was vitally important no one discover us. The solution, we thought, was for Macy to flirt with and pretend to date the guys that asked her out. Problems developed on her dates when drinking and dancing and intimate conversation led to fooling around with boys in cars and then escalated into much more than fooling around. Normally that would end a relationship. However, we discovered that I am an extreme voyeur and the next thing you know, I am hiding in our closet secretly watching Macy get fucked by another guy.

It hurt and it made me jealous and it was really difficult to watch, but for some reason I also found watching her wildly exciting and erotic.

It pushed buttons for Macy too. She loved the attention and being so intensely desired by other men, but she also loved what it did to me, and she loved the select freedom of

2

acting slutty without judgment. We both got caught up and swept along by it. By the time it all ended Macy and I had learned lots of new things about us. We facetiously refer to it as her 'flirtatious adventure'.

In the days and weeks afterwards our sex was insane. We had consumed rocket-fuel right from the nozzle. We fucked all the time, everywhere, and Macy could not get enough of my dick in her mouth. Macy never did anything with another guy but she would flirt like crazy and I always got so hot. Every time she did it was a reminder of what she had done. The anguish and jealousy were still there but they just seemed to throw gasoline on my fire. I don't know why I loved seeing her behave so sexually, I just did.

I realized she was actually waiting for an answer. Boyfriends and husbands were not allowed at the expo while the girls were working. I would drop her off in the morning and pick her up in the evening and that was all the contact I was allowed to have. The clock was ticking on my visit to this dressing room with her. Once the show started, I'd be kicked out. So did I actually want her to flirt? As always, the thought was exciting and torturous. But how would I feel so cut off and excluded?

"No," I concluded. "I suppose not. I have to go all day without seeing you. I may not even get a text or call. I'd be too much of an outsider. I think it'd be more frustrating than exciting. Better you just do your job and work the booth. I'll wander and try to see as much of this place as I can and kill time until I see you at night."

The expo itself was huge; thousands of vendors and tens of thousands of participants. The over-all umbrella was sport and fitness but all types of businesses joined in. Shane hawked an energy drink called "Enjoy" that claimed to boost your workout yet help you sleep. It must work because his sales had taken off. The fact that he only hired gorgeous, super-fit, hot-body, big-tit, cheerleader types to work his booths may have helped his business plan. It sure didn't hurt it.

Macy was scrutinizing me.

"What?" I asked.

3

Macy shrugged. "Nothing," she muttered. "It's just that your eyes didn't match your words. But if you don't want me to flirt, I won't."

"Thank you."

She looked down at the ring I had so recently placed on her finger.

"It does make it even more exciting though, doesn't it? Being engaged? I'm engaged to marry you yet flirting with another man. I feel so much naughtier when I do it now. Let me know if you change your mind."

Macy knew my buttons so well. This was all still new to us so uncertainty lingered about where the boundaries were and how far was too far. What Macy was naive to was her own sex appeal; her big hazel eyes were born containing a promise of more. I've seen her talk to countless men and every one of them fell under her spell. She exceptionally pretty but it's more than that; something in her eyes tells you that you have a chance. Her body is built for sex. Her breasts are a little too big for her size and her arms make contact with them often, moving them around under her clothes. She's an athlete; gymnastics in high school and a gym-rat now. Her butt bubbles out like two halves of a volley-ball.

Best of all, she's blithely unaware of it. She's not stupid or dingy; she knows males and a lot of females react to her. But that knowledge has never made it in to her paradigm for living. She's always pleasantly surprised when the next person finds her attractive too. She never vainly expects it.

Across the dressing room we heard Shane barge in and start telling the girls "ten minutes, wrap up whatever you're doing we go live in ten minutes." Macy leaned in and kissed me and I squeezed her muscular ass in those ridiculous tight shorts.

"Knock them dead," I said.

***

Three hours later I decided to risk a look at Macy's booth. If Shane saw me she'd get in trouble so I bought some Oakley sunglasses and an Under-Armour wind breaker and

4

slowly worked my way around until I saw her booth. There were six girls working it at the moment. All the girls rotated through each position each shift; stage, table, aisle. Macy was behind a table distributing information. I hid by another booth and pretended to be interested in some vitamins.

A booming laugh brought my head up. The booth next to Shane's was a new company called "Big Brothas" selling inter-locking free weights. They had installed an Olympic bench and dumbbells on their stage and four huge black guys were going through their workout routine dressed only in baggy black shorts, red high-top Reebok sneakers, and tank-tops that had so much room around the arms and neck they hung all the way down to their abs.

These guys were massive. Obviously professional body-builders, they had muscles stacked on top of their muscles. Their trapezoids flared out into swollen, rounded deltoids. Their arms were bigger than my legs and covered with jagged veins. As the guys moved through their routine and pumped up, they grew even bigger.

The laughter came from one of the guys talking to one of Shane's girls up on stage. I worried for a second it was Macy but my fiancée was too busy ignoring those muscle-bound goofs. Arrogant, cocky men like that are a big turn-off for her. I should have known better. Egocentric males always turn Macy cold. There was no way guys like this would ever get to her.

The girl up on stage seemed to be enjoying herself very much however. The body-builder she was talking to had dreadlocks half-way down his back and teeth so white I saw them glowing. She kept squeezing his giant biceps and pounding on his rock-hard chest. He boomed another big laugh. She was a giggling ant attacking an elephant.

When I looked back at Macy she was talking to an older gentleman wearing an olive suit. She was flipping through the informational brochures and earnestly educating him on the many health benefits of "Enjoy". I decided I'd seen enough and turned to walk away but just as I did Macy dropped her pen and bent over to retrieve it. Even from this distance the view down the front of her V-neck was spectacular, and I was sure that olive suit was thanking God for being in the right place at the right time. I saw his whole body stiffen. When Macy stood up she looked into his eyes somewhat knowingly and I realized she was flirting with him regardless of our agreement. I was irritated and yet aroused.

Ten minutes later I was seated at Jack in the Box laughing at myself.

Really? That irritated me? I thought back on some of the things I had recently seen Macy do and now I was irritated because she flashed her cleavage at some old guy? Besides, what was I going to do, admit I was spying on her?

I took a bite of my hamburger and told myself to shut the fuck up. After I ate I cut back through the big hall and noticed all the girls had rotated positions again and now Macy was up on stage completely ignoring the big black guys all trying to talk to her. I smiled and went to watch Captain America; Winter Soldier alone then went to the park by the lake and fed the ducks.

I was walking downtown, still killing time and just getting a feel for this big city, when my phone buzzed. Macy text I didn't need to pick her up from the expo because Shane was taking all the girls out for drinks for doing such a great job day one. She would meet me back at our motel room in a few hours. I let her know it was no problem, be safe, have fun. If she needed me to come pick her up later I would.

*** 

Four hours later I still hadn't heard from her. I'd sent her two texts and called her twice but her phone went straight to voice mail. I was about to call her again when I heard a car pull up out front. I peeked through the gap in the tacky black-out drapes and saw Macy exit a red Mercedes sedan with tinted windows. Shane drove a classic Camaro. Four girls got out of the car with her and everybody changed seats. The girls still wore their expo outfits. All the girls hugged and said their goodbyes talking a hundred miles an hour.

I composed myself and quickly sat on the foot of the bed. Macy slipped her card in and the door opened and as

6

soon as she saw me she smiled and dropped her bags and skipped over to me, jumping onto my lap.

"Hi Honey!" she chirped.

I gave her my best stern look. "Macy, where have you been? You said a few hours and it's been over four. I was worried. Why is your phone off?"

Her eyes grew big.

"Is it? Shit! I'm so sorry!" She fumbled through one of her bags until she found it. "I'm so sorry Honey. I thought I turned it back on after the show. I figured since you didn't call or text you were busy at the movies or something. Time flew by. I had no idea I was gone so long. I'm so sorry."

I may have been looking into her eyes but really I was using all my senses to see if anything other than drinks and conversation had taken place. I was unable to detect anything unusual. Nothing had happened.

"Where did you all go?" I asked.

She hesitated. Boom! Something had happened!

"We started at the bar attached to the convention center but after a while some of the other guys wanted to go back to their room."

"Guys?"

She looked away from me and around the room.

I just stared, waiting for her to go on. After a moment or two she did.

"Some of the girls had swapped numbers with these big black guys working the booth next to ours and must have text them. Next thing I know all four of them show up. We all drank and talked and after a few hours Shane took off. The guys said let's go back to our hotel room so we did; six of us girls and all four of them. I didn't do anything with them Honey, I swear."

"What did happen? What did you do? You were gone over four hours Sweetheart."

"One of the guys, Darryl, stayed on the couch talking to me. We talked about everything. The girls all paired off with the guys and started making out. Stacey sat on Dereck's lap and the other two guys had two girls each on them. It was obvious the alcohol was really getting to everyone."

"Is Darryl good looking?"

She shrugged. "In a rugged way. He shaves his head and has a big gold-loop earring. It's not his looks though, it's his confidence. I bet he's never been scared or intimidated in his life. He's as big as a Grizzly bear but instead of feeling afraid of him I felt safe. The more I talked to him the better looking he got. Does that happen to you Sweetie? Can a girl get more attractive by talking to her?"

"Sometimes. Go on, what else happened?"

"It quickly got pretty intense. Dereck fucked Stacey there on the couch. The other four girls sucked off both guys right in front of everyone. It was really hot. Honey, all five of those girls have husbands or boyfriends. Girls are just as bad as boys; they just keep it to themselves. Boys brag."

"But you somehow behaved yourself?"

"Don't be like that. Yes, I behaved myself. I told you I would and I did. I have to admit it wasn't easy. I got really horny. Those guys are huge *everywhere*. The girls looked like children next to them, so tiny. Darryl didn't even try anything. I leaned my back against his chest to watch the others and we both got warm and started breathing hard, but he was a total gentleman."

Angst rose in my throat. I pictured the scene perfectly and hell yes it was hot. I really liked that Macy had witnessed it all and that it had turned her on. I know she felt bad for being out so long and I wondered if she was still horny and just hiding it.

I tested her by pulling down the front of my shorts. As soon as she saw my dick she dropped to her knees between my legs and sucked like a whore, really working the shaft and head. Yup, she was still horny. I tossed her up on the bed onto all fours and pulled her shorts to the side and fucked her like I had just bought her. She climaxed hard and fast and so did I.

\*\*\*

We woke late the next morning and she had to run around like crazy to get ready on time. We barely made it. I dropped her at the show then spent the morning killing time

8

again and then went back to the motel room for a nap. That's when I spotted her phone. In our rush she'd forgotten it. I tried to calculate a plan to get it back to her when I noticed the little green light blinking telling her she had a text. I admit it took me two seconds, maybe less, to decide to read it.

"Great getting to know you last night, looking forward to knowing you better - D"

So Macy had given her number to Darryl. Jealous rage flared up in me. I considered all the mean and terrible things I would say to her. After a few minutes of fuming, I began to settle down.

I immediately felt shitty. I searched for a way to mark it as 'unread' but failed to find it. Do I delete it and let Darryl and Macy figure out what happened to it or do I give her back her phone with the message read and tell her I thought it was from her trying to draw my attention to her phone? I pictured Macy leaning against Darryl last night watching others have sex and hit delete. Fuck that. Maybe Darryl would conclude Macy was ignoring him.

Minutes later the phone in the motel room rang. It was Macy. She asked me if her phone was there and when I said yes she asked me to sneak it in to her. I said I would.

I made my way back to the convention hall and entered through the loading docks in back, just like yesterday, but this time I noticed maintenance stored big trash-cans on wheels and brooms. Off to the side on wire racks were uniforms and cleanser. I grabbed some green overalls and a hat, stuffed some brooms in a trash can and walked out like I owned the place right onto the exhibition floor. Some douche dropped a coffee cup into my trash can less than a minute later. I strolled up and down a few rows, working my way over to Macy. I might as well have been invisible.

As I rounded a corner I saw the Big Brothas booth. Today their uniform was a super-tight red T-shirt and black bicycle shorts. They still wore the red Reeboks. I noticed the guy with the dreads, Dereck. He's the one that fucked Stacey. If I was going to fuck any of the girls Macy worked with, it would be Stacey. She has long dark hair and a body almost as good as Macy's.

A few more steps and now Macy's booth was before me as well. Macy was talking to a customer. I looked at the six girls and four guys and my secret knowledge of how they all spent their evening together was very exciting.

I was a little conflicted about the fact that all of the girls had boyfriends or husbands. It was none of my business and I don't know what the rules were for their relationships; maybe fucking and sucking black body builders was okay. But still, I doubted it, and I felt bad for them.

As I emptied a small wastebasket, Stacey's husband discreetly walked by and smiled and Stacey beamed with pleasure at seeing him. Poor guy, he has no idea what his wife did last night. But that thought made me wonder; do I know for sure what my fiancée did last night? Would Macy fool around and not tell me? I just didn't think so. After how truthful she'd been through her 'flirtatious adventure', why lie now? She knows I have a weird kink about her acting slutty. If she told me she had slipped up last night with Darryl, there was a good chance we wouldn't even fight about it. In my gut I knew nothing had happened.

But how would I feel if something had? I had to stop and think about this. My reaction was two-fold; first, Macy lying to me would not be okay. We don't work like that and she knows how I feel, so there's no reason for her to. If she did I'd be hurt and angry. Second, the idea of her pinned down under one of those huge black, muscular bodies was pretty fucking hot. This happened to me every time. I'm so conflicted. I want her to do something more than flirting and I dread her doing something more than flirting.

I looked up in time to see Stacey's husband exit the hall. He must have just come by to say hello. How sweet. Back at the booth I saw Dereck give Stacey a knowing smile and she actually blushed. I gave her the once over again. Fuck, what a babe. I bet Dereck really enjoyed himself.

Macy had finished with her customer and a giant black man with shaved head and gold earring was talking to her and I guessed that must be Darryl. I moved a little closer but behind a partition so I could hear them talking.

"I told you I'm engaged," Macy said.

"I heard you, but that still doesn't answer my question; do you want to come back to our room again tonight or not?"

Macy rolled her eyes.

"Okay, fine. No, I don't. Does that answer your question?"

Daryl smiled broadly. "You're such a bad liar."

I had to agree with him, she really was. She clearly wanted to hang out with him again tonight, which surprised me because normally muscle-bound guys were at the bottom of her list. She'd pick a guy that collected comic books over an egotistical, self-centered gym-rat every time. Darryl must have a brain and some heart too.

"Anyway, Little Miss Engaged," he continued. "Here's a spare room key. We'll be back at our suite after dinner, around eight."

Macy's mouth fell open when Darryl pushed the plastic card into her palm.

"I can't take this!" Macy said, but she made no move to give it back or drop it in the trash. Darryl just grinned displaying two rows of perfect white teeth.

"See you after eight," he laughed and moved back on stage and grabbed some dumbbells.

Exasperated, Macy stamped her foot, but after a minute she slipped the key-card into the waistband of her little shorts.

When she walked over to talk to one of the other girls, I placed her cell phone on the table by the brochures. I knew she'd see it soon or one of her friends would and recognize it and give it to her.

I moved as slowly and deliberately as possible and then calmly left the area. Back at the loading dock I slipped out of the overalls and walked to Jack in the Box again and just as I got in line, my phone buzzed with a text.

"WTF? How did you do that???"

I text back, "I have Ninja powers. See you at six o'clock."

Then I held my breath. Would she hang out with me tonight? Would she sneak away to Darryl's? Would she ask if she could go and maybe invite me along? She text back a "thank you Sweetie" and that was the last I heard from her for a long time. I ended up killing the whole day exploring the city again.

As time passed my excitement grew. I wanted her to want to go back to their room. By late afternoon I was even considering telling her I was at a movie and I might not get back to the motel room until well after ten o'clock. That would almost force her to go to Darryl's room. I rejected that idea because it made me feel like I was causing it to happen instead of her choosing for it to happen.

At five-forty five I received a text; "Pick me up at the loading dock. I'll be there in ten minutes. Miss you!"

So my sweet baby girl was going to be loyal. I felt relief but if I'm honest I also felt disappointment. What the hell's wrong with me?

I was there a few minutes early and when she came walking down the ramp my breath caught in my throat. She's so gorgeous. The wind swirled her hair and her full breasts bounced under her shirt. Her thighs flexed with each step. She was a vision of feminine strength and grace and she was in love with me. Pride and adrenaline surged through me. When she saw me a huge smile spread across her face and I suddenly felt stupid for even considering she go back to their room. Why would I ever allow another man to touch her? I cherished her. When offered something else she had chosen me and I felt foolish and lame for contemplating sharing her. I got out and walked to meet her and we kissed, happy and in love. I opened the door for her and once we were both inside she said she was starving so I drove to a restaurant I had seen while out that day. She put on a knee-length coat and tied it at the waist before entering.

She told me about her day and I told her about mine. Except for Stacey, when the guys had asked for a repeat performance from the girls they had declined. The alcohol had worn off and guilt had kicked in. Stacey on the other hand had been all for it and had told her husband there was a quick after-show team meeting and had taken Dereck back-stage and given him a blowjob before leaving to meet her husband. I asked if Stacey and her husband had an understanding and Macy said no, Stacey was doing all this behind his back.

12

I'm so fucked up. What Macy was sharing about Stacey actually turned me on. Sex-loving women are awesome. I pictured Macy behaving like this instead of Stacey. Before I could stop myself I asked Macy if she wanted to suck Darryl's cock too. I heard the words come out of my mouth and then braced myself for her irritation. Macy sat her Pepsi back on the table and studied me. What she said next surprised me.

"Can I? Would that be okay with you?"

Now it was my turn to study her. Was she fucking with me or was she being boldly serious? She had on her best poker face because I couldn't tell one way or the other. Unsure what direction to take, I waited her out. At last the expected irritation appeared.

"I don't get you James," she began. "One minute it seems like you are all into the idea of me with another man again and then the next minute you seem so relieved when nothing happens. You are sending me mixed signals Babe. I'm about ready to take the idea off the table permanently; we can just go back to the way we were before I fooled around with those other guys. I suspect you wouldn't actually like that and neither would I but this is all too confusing."

"I know Mace, and you're totally one hundred percent right. I'm a mess about this stuff. I desperately want it and I'm totally fearful of it. I have no excuse or explanation. What do you want? Tell me the hard truth Honey."

"No way. You're not putting all this on my shoulders. If things went bad and feelings got hurt, you'd lay it all at my feet."

She was right. I was trying to take the easy way out. I had to look inside myself and sort out all my mixed emotions and then share them with her. The task seemed insurmountable. I knew one thing for sure and I needed to hear it from her.

"Macy, one of my biggest fears is that you would do something that you didn't really want to do just to please me or make me happy. I can't stand that idea. Promise me anything and everything you do springs from your own desire for it. This includes our entire relationship, not just this kinky sex stuff."

"I promise Honey. That's an easy one."

13

"Okay, good. So, knowing that and trusting you on that I have to ask, just so I know we are starting with a blank slate; have you already ever done that?"

"Yes."

My heart sank.

"When?"

"Last year's Super Bowl. We went to PT's Pub with your friends from work. I hated it and didn't want to go but I knew how happy it would make you to have a girl that shared your love of football, so I went and acted interested. I'm really not."

I laughed. "That's it?" I asked.

"Yup."

"Jacob? Austin? All those guys? You did all that just for you?"

"Hell yes and I loved it. I'd do it again. Are you kidding me? Baby that was the sexiest thing ever! I had all these hot guys chasing me and I actually got to have sex with a few of them, all while I had an amazing man at home totally in love with me. I got the best of both worlds. It was fantastic!"

Her enthusiasm was exciting. I remembered some of the scenes from those times and felt my penis swell.

"But Honey," she went on. "It was only so exciting because it was all in addition to having a relationship with you. If I didn't have you in my life I'd never act like that. Do you understand? I don't know why you reacted the way you did but I trust it. I've heard about guys like you. If I ever for even a split second thought that my actions would actually hurt you, like in a real and serious way, I'd stop in an instant."

She stopped talking long enough for a family to walk past and then continued.

"I'd never do it to make you happy. I do it for me. But it only works for me so long as I'm with you. "

I was nodding my head in understanding. I believed her and that was a tremendous relief. I found her excitement arousing but needed to know it was genuine. She had convinced me it was.

"So," she stated. "Now you know how I feel. Tell me what you are so afraid of."

14

I fidgeted for a moment, nervous about what I wanted to say. Finally I just said it.

"Losing you, Macy. Some big-dick stud fucking you so well you fall in love with him and forget all about me, and I'm the biggest fool in the world because I let my super-hot fiancée fuck him in the first place. But actually it would be worse than that because I didn't just let you, I encouraged you. In fact, I practically held your legs open for him."

"You think I'm super-hot?"

It drives me crazy when she does that, which is why she does it.

"Yes! My god look at you! Your body is like a gymnast crossed with a cheerleader; it's perfect. Your face is a Maxim cover. You love sex and as we both so recently discovered, you kind of have a thing for bigger than average penises. How am I ever going to keep all those men away from you? It's daunting and intimidating. I love that other men want you but for fuck's sake, ALL the other men want you. Even women want you. I'm not rich or famous or a genius or even all that buff. I'm just me. You're a goddess."

She was laughing at me. Not a cruel or hurtful laugh, but a soft and understanding laugh.

"Baby," she said. "I may not agree with your assessment of me but I love that you have it. It is true that sex almost always bring emotional attachment for women and I've admitted to you what happened with Jacob gave me a little crush on him. I still feel something for him. But nothing touches what we have Sweetie. I wish there was something I could say that would allow you to see into my heart. You'd know then how solid we are. I love you because of who you are; not what you have. I'm specifically in love with you, the person. Nothing can touch or change that."

Something in her tone caught at me. I met her eyes, her big hazel eyes. She was so open, so earnest. We could do this, I realized. We could play this dangerous game and be okay. We could walk right along the cliff's edge and come away unscathed. She had met my insecurities and reassured me. With almost all the fear stripped away, I discovered I was incredibly turned on and getting more aroused by the minute. When she spoke next, her voice was a raspy whisper.

"It's your turn Lover; is this extra, kinky element part of our relationship or not? Are you in or out, once and for all? "

My heart was racing. I wasn't sure what I was agreeing to, exactly, but it felt big and important. Under the table my penis pulsed in time with my heart beat.

"I'm in," I breathed. My mouth was so dry.

"Good. Me too. Kiss me."

I did. Not too much though, it was a family restaurant.

I expected her to reach for her phone and text Darryl she'd make eight o'clock after all, but she didn't. In fact, she said nothing more about it so I didn't either and we had a delightful and intimate diner. We laughed and told each other stories and I remembered all the special connections we shared that made this relationship so extraordinary. By the time the check came we had fallen even more deeply in love.

All our talk about my kink had gotten me really hot and I was eager to get her back to the motel room. On the drive back she took my hand and placed it inside her jacket and against her left breast. I took her hand and placed it on my erection. By the time we stepped inside our room and closed the door I thought we'd be after each other like animals. Macy had other ideas.

"Doesn't the Jacuzzi sound perfect right now? My whole body aches from standing all day. Let's change into our suits and go down to the pool."

I was frustrated and let it show on my face. She chuckled and walked to the bathroom, dropping clothes as she went. When she returned she wore a new black one-piece swimsuit cut low in front but especially low under the arms. About a third of each breast was exposed all along the side until they curved away. The back was open all the way down to the two dimples just above her ass. She looked smoking hot. I wanted to throw her onto our bed. As fast as I could I changed clothes and grabbed a towel. As I approached her she placed a gentle hand on my chest. I looked at her confused.

"I have another idea," she said. She leaned in close, pressed her firm breasts against my chest. Faint spearmint rose to my nostrils. She'd brushed her teeth while in the bathroom. "Give me fifteen minutes and then come down. Let's act like we don't know each other. Nobody at this motel has seen us together because I've been working so much. This is a great opportunity for me to flirt right in front of you."

My temperature rose fifteen degrees. My balls tightened.

"Okay," I said. "I'll bring my phone, like I'm waiting for someone to join me. I'll just gawk at you like I'm sure every other guy down there will do."

She laughed once and gave me a peck on the lips, grabbed her things and zipped out the door. Just for good measure, and to prove to myself that I could, I waited almost thirty minutes instead of fifteen. Consequently, when I arrived at the dimly lit Jacuzzi Macy was already engaged in conversation with two middle-aged men. Neither had a remarkable body or was particularly good looking. I said hi to everybody and dropped my towel in a chair. I entered the water slowly because it was scalding

Macy had chosen her seat well. The step she was on allowed the water to just reach the bottom of her boobs. She had already dipped her head under at least once as all that thick dark hair was plastered down her back. With it pulled back like that you could really see how striking her features were; high cheek bones and slight nose separating her over-sized and expressive green eyes. She barely glanced at me. There was no way anybody could tell we were together. After a few minutes I rose up and sat on the edge, then dried my hands and reached for my phone. I just surfed the news but acted like I was busy texting someone.

The men were really attentive to Macy, hanging on every word she said. After a while she moved a little farther out of the water and now the soaked fabric hung down even lower; the hefty curve of her under-breast was visible. I caught them devouring every inch of her every time she looked down at the water.

17

After a while she excused herself to go jump in the regular pool to cool off. She was gone less than ten minutes but when she came back I noticed she had re-tied her top strap. Now her scoop neck hung almost down to her nipples and her side and bottom breasts were almost busting out. The thin material was vacuum sealed to her hips and vulva because of the water. She was killing me and killing both her admirers too.

One of the guys got up and went to his stuff on a chair. He came back with a joint and a lighter. When he sat down this time he was half way between Macy and the other guy. He took a hit and offered it to the other guy who also took a hit, and then he offered it to my fiancée.

*Oh boy,* I thought, *here we go.*

She took a long drag and held her breath, passing it back to him. He looked at me with a question but I waved him off. When he offered it to her again he didn't reach his arm out as far so Macy scooted closer to get it and took another big hit. The three of them started talking softer and they all got back in the hot water.

I laughed as if I had just read a funny text and they were oblivious. None of them even glanced at me. In less than a minute they had floated close enough to each other that their knees were most likely touching under water. They were talking low enough now I could only catch the occasional word.

Then I heard Macy gasp.

I managed to control my reaction and look up slowly. I didn't want them to know I'd heard. Macy was now seated between them with her head tilted back on the edge of the hot tub and her eyes closed. I suspected that the guy on her right was playing with her breasts under the churning water but was the guy on her left fingering her? I couldn't tell for sure under the suds but by the way his body was turned just a little and his shoulder was moving it sure looked like it.

When the two of them turned to face Macy more she kind of realized what was happening and opened her eyes and stood in the center of the tub. Her top looked a little stretched but was still covering her tits. She glanced at me

18

and I saw the desire in her eyes. Our talk at dinner, the weed, her new friends touching her under the water; my sweet Macy was ready to pop.

I was busy trying to think of something clever to say that would let her know I wanted her to head back to our room when the guy with the weed turned her by the shoulder and walked her backwards towards his lap. Macy was looking at me the whole way.

He reached around to her mouth and held what was left of the joint to her lips and as she took a hit she settled her hips back into his. Whatever I was about to say died on my tongue. While he held the roach to her lips with one hand, with the other he pulled her tit out the side of her top and squeezed her breast. She was too big for his hand and I saw his fingers denting her boob. When he lightly pinched her nipple she moaned a little and fell back against his body.

Voices from the gate made us all look. Two couples, all of the around forty, made their way toward the hot tub, towels and clothes draped over their arms. With a mischievous smile Macy nestled her body up against Weed Guy and sank low into the water. Her freed breast no longer visible.

The two couples took up open positions around the edge and said all their hellos to us. Soon everyone, except me, was engaged in small talk. I'm certain they all thought Macy and Weed Guy were a couple, which really got under my skin but turned me on. After about ten minutes of this Macy surprised me by turning her body enough to kiss Weed Guy on the lips. For a second I worried she was going to flash everyone her naked tit but it was safely back in place by now. The kiss was tender and passionate. I felt my penis move. When it ended Macy settled back down onto his lap again in a somewhat new position, making it easier to kiss him a few more times. Once she even laid her head on his chest like she was dizzy.

About thirty minutes later the foursome decided to call it a night. After good-nights all around, they gathered their belongings and left. Macy made out with Weed Guy for a little while longer and then announced she was tired and headed to

19

bed, raised a secret eyebrow at me, pulled herself out of the tub and left. The older guys left separately. I was alone.

After what I guessed to be long enough for Macy to get back to our room and the other guys to get back to theirs, I collected my things and left.

When I opened the door to our room Macy was naked and lying on her back, cupping both breasts, with her pussy aimed at the front door. I don't know what my expression was but she laughed at it. I stripped and crawled up between her legs, gazing into her eyes, and we began kissing. Goddamn that girl can kiss. Her make-out session with Weed Guy had us both hot and we attacked each other. I roughly mauled her left tit and she moaned so I pinched her hard nipple and then sucked it into my hot mouth. She started working her hips against me so I knew she wanted dick so while keeping her nipple in my mouth I raised up on my knees and lined myself up and pushed my penis inside her.

It slid in remarkably easy. I mean *really* easily. She was already soaking wet and I wondered if the Jacuzzi water was making her slick. She was also really warm, much warmer than usual. Her pussy was actually hot. I pumped her a few times, pushing in as far as I could. Her eyes were wild and dancing and almost seemed to glow. She was so slippery I was actually losing some sensation. I looked into her eyes and pumped her faster. She smiled.

"You're so wet."

"Am I?" Her eyes were laughing.

I lifted myself to my fists and began thrusting harder into her. She moaned and put both hands on my shoulders. I started pounding her. She bit her bottom lip and told me to fuck her harder. I looked down at the joining of our bodies, watching my shaft piston in and out.

My dick was covered in semen.

I jerked my eyes up to hers. She moved her hands behind my neck and pulled my ear down to her lips.

"Fuck your dirty fiancée Baby. Add your cum to his."

A million volts jolted my body. *He had fucked her? In the Jacuzzi? Right in front of all of us?* My dick surged and hardened and Macy felt it and groaned.

20

"You love it, don't you James? He played with my tits and I felt him get hard and he pulled it out under the water and pulled my suit to the side and when I felt his head against my lips I pushed my hips down onto him. God! His fat cock felt so good. I loved fucking him right in front of you Baby. I loved fucking him in front of everyone. You didn't even know, did you? It was so hot. I leaned my head against his chest when I came. I came so hard! He gave me no time to recover. Older men are awesome. They have so much control. He barely moved his hips at all and it drove me insane. Finally I felt him swell really big and explode, pumping his sperm deep inside me. I'm such a slut!"

Her words were driving me crazy. I remembered everything and now knowing he had been inside her all that time was too much. With a loud groan my hips jerked and a spasm shook them and I shot my cum into my fiancée, adding my load to his inside her. I collapsed on the bed next to her. She wrapped her fingers around my messy penis and stroked a few times and my super-sensitivity made it almost too much to take. She slid down the bed and took me into her hot mouth, tasting both of us. She sucked hard, pulling out my last few drops and causing intense shivers up and down my spine. I couldn't take it and had to push her mouth off of me. She snuggled up under my chin and against my chest. She was smirking.

Once I caught my breath I was finally able to speak.

"You fucked him?"

"Yes, my Love, I did. Your hard dick tells me you approve."

I thought of a few contradictory responses but seriously, what could I say? My hard dick rendered any argument void. No matter what I said to the contrary, deep down, I obviously liked it.

"I'm a little scared to admit it but yes, I approve."

"I'm so happy to hear you say that." She leaned up and gave me a salty kiss. "I was going to just give him a blowjob on the edge of the Jacuzzi right in front of you but he had other ideas. God, I love it when men want me so badly. I'm such a sucker for desire."

We lay in silence for a while. I looked down the length of her tone, athletic body. One big tit rested on my chest, her hips rose and flared before transforming into a strong thigh hooked around my leg. Her delicate foot played with my masculine one.

"Men can't resist you, Mace. You're Eve. Women either, but seeing you with a woman would do nothing for me."

"Me either. I love men. Women are beautiful and sexy but I love cock. I love the way they look and feel. Some can be ugly but mostly I find them fascinating and captivating and masculine and powerful, and the bigger the better."

"Bigger...and black?"

I felt her relaxed body stiffen a little against me.

"Would that bother you?" she asked.

I considered for a moment. "No," I answered. "In fact, the more I think about it, the hotter I get. You would look so sexy up against Darryl's big, black body. Would it excite you more because he's black?"

I felt her shiver.

"Yes. Very much." She was trying hard to maintain control and that told me she found the idea wildly erotic. Macy grew up in a small, all-white town in Southern California. All through school she never shared a classroom with a black child. I imagined black men were probably pretty exotic to her.

"Ask me for permission," I told her.

Her eyebrows lifted. I'd caught her by surprise but she joined right in.

"James, my wonderful fiancé, may I please seduce Darryl? I really want him to fuck me but I need your permission first."

I pondered her question.

"That depends," I said.

"On what Darling?"

"On how big his dick is. No little dicks for my Baby. I know what she likes."

"Oh, no worries Honey, he's big."

She said it with such conviction it was as if she were stating a fact. Was she that good an actress or did she actually know? Had something happened between them although she had told me otherwise? If I questioned her and I was wrong, if she was just playing along with my little game, I looked like an insecure, distrusting asshole. As luck would have it, I didn't have to decide whether or not to question her. When she saw my brain working she realized she'd made a mistake and quickly confessed.

"I'm so sorry Honey. I know I should have told you. I just got so nervous I said the wrong thing and then because I'd said the wrong thing I couldn't go back and say the right thing because that would make me a liar."

I sat up in bed and looked at her.

"So what *did* happen?"

Don't worry; it was just a little white lie. That night when I was leaning back against him and we were watching everyone around us have sex, Darryl got really hard and asked if he could take it out because his shorts were hurting him. I wanted to see it so of course I said yes. You know how guys are. He took that and ran with it. In seconds he was totally nude and stroking as he watched my friends fuck and suck his friends. I leaned back up against him but honestly, I watched him more than I watched them."

"Well?"

"Well what Honey?"

"What did he look like? Was he big? What about his body?"

"His body was amazing. I couldn't make a steady diet of all those muscles but he sure would make a fantastic snack. His thighs are as big as my torso. His arms are bigger than my legs. Every square inch of him is as hard as granite. He is so *male*."

She pulled me back down and snuggled me again.

"James," she breathed, "His cock is gorgeous. It's thick and long, but has this graceful curve up and away from his lap that leaves my pussy tingling. It's like I can already feel it inside me and I know It will feel amazing. But that's not all; his testicles are big too, way bigger than yours Honey." She held up her two fists next to each other. "His balls are bigger than my two fists Lover, and he's completely hairless all over. I wanted to lick every inch of him. He's an onyx god."

23

"And you want to fuck him?"

"With your permission."

"What if I said no?"

Macy studied my face. I didn't dare tell her but I was hoping she'd admit she would fuck him anyway. I know that's perverse, but I wanted it. I wanted her to want him so badly she would ignore my wishes. I loved the thought of my sweet Macy that hot for cock. I wanted her willing to cheat on me to get it. She saw right through me.

"I'd fuck him anyway."

My penis twitched and she saw it. She smiled. She had me now. She reached down and cupped my balls.

"His would overflow my hand Honey. I'd need both hands to hold his. Can you imagine how much sperm they contain? I can. Maybe I'll fuck him and not tell you, like I just did that guy in the Jacuzzi. You didn't get angry, you got turned on."

My penis started to grow and harden.

"You're doing it again right now. You like that idea. Would you like to know how much cum he shot out that night Honey? I put my face right down there next to his dick, you know. I wanted to see it all. He was a fountain of sperm, a huge black hose spraying long frosty ropes of white jizz all over the rug."

I moaned and she moved her hand from my balls to my shaft. I had gotten hard fast and Macy started stroking me.

"It was exciting to watch but you know what else I felt? Disappointment. What a waste. The woman in me cried out at such a loss. Every drop of that should have gone right up inside me. My mouth watered watching that huge, powerful man taking care of himself like that. I could spend an hour just sucking on his big thing."

I couldn't take any more. I started shooting out all over my stomach. Macy chuckled with glee at what she had made me do. She milked me like a cow. We lay there in silence for a long time. I was waiting for her to tell me she was going to meet him at his room. A glance at the clock on the nightstand showed me it was just a little before eight o'clock.

Something I've come to understand about myself is that this kink of mine grows in strength and power until I orgasm and then it drops way down. Before I cum I'm ready to hand Macy over to another man but after I cum I get protective and selfish and needy and scared. At the moment I was feeling all those things. But things had shifted for Macy and me. We had talked frankly about the rules and the expectations and we had both agreed we were fully invested. I couldn't go chicken-shit on her now. So I waited and kept my mouth shut and prepared myself for whatever she wanted to say. When she finally said it, I wasn't prepared. Not at all.

"Honey, let's shower and get dressed. I really want to fuck Darryl but I want you to meet him first."

To my credit, I handled it really well.

"No," I refused. "I don't give you permission."

Macy's eyes flared and for a split-second she was angry, but then she understood.

"Okay Baby," she purred. "But I'm going anyway. I want him so badly I'm going to ignore your wishes. I'm so hot for his big black cock. I'd prefer not to cheat on you but if that's how you're going to be, then you get to watch me walk out the door without you."

She got up and headed for the bathroom. I rolled onto my back dreading what I had done and seriously questioning my sanity.

Watching her get ready was excruciating. Every little thing she did to herself, I knew she was doing for him. Of course she shaved, but this time she shaved completely. Usually she kept a small patch above her clit. She placed little dabs of perfume, not just behind her ears but behind her knees and trailing down her stomach to her pussy. The outfit she chose; Black patent leather boot that came up past her knees, short black, pleated mini-skirt that barely covered her young, firm ass which she wrapped in shear black-lace panties, and a fuzzy teal button-up long sleeve sweater, so tight it looked painted on. Beneath it she wore no bra. The little bumps of her nipples were already visible without being hard. Every choice well thought out and calculated to maximize her appeal and attractiveness. By the time she was ready my balls were aching.

I sat on the foot of the bed in my robe watching her prepare for her date. She loved it. I couldn't hide the desire in my eyes any more than I could hide the agony and anguish there, and she loved that too. At last she came and stood before me. Her back arched and her ass jutted out. Her big firm breasts stretched her sweater and strained at the fabric. She was close enough to me her legs were between my knees. I reached for her but she gently steered my hand away and held it.

"I have to tell you," she admitted. "This is all made more exciting by your refusal. I like that I'm doing this against your will. It's really empowering. My man is telling me no yet I'm doing it anyway. I'm a bad girl."

She stepped closer and nudged my legs farther apart.

"I'm already so wet."

She moved closer still, forcing me wider, wide enough to be uncomfortable.

"I want to be alone with Darryl, but I don't want to deny myself the pleasure of your audience. What to do, what to do? Then I thought of a plan."

She turned my hand over and placed a plain white plastic card in it.

That is the room key to Darryl's suite. He's staying at the Hyatt just down the street. He passed it to me earlier today. I wasn't going to use it but the hours since he gave it to me have been illuminating and educational. Funny thing is, I'm still not going to use it."

She dropped to her knees and opened my robe, allowing my penis and testicles to hang in the open air. She leaned in to kiss my shaft but didn't. She was so close I felt her hot breath. I looked down into her teasing eyes.

"I'm not going to use it because you are. I know which room number is his. I'm going up to his room and I'll knock on his door and he'll let me in. Then I'll explain that my fiancé has his room key and will be joining us later, to watch. After I've spent some alone time with Darryl, I'll call you and let you know which room number is his and you can come up and join

26

us. Unless you don't want to, in which case I'll be back whenever I'm back."

The entire time she was telling me her plan, she moved her mouth and lips and hot breath all around my penis without touching it. It was torture. Have I created a monster or just set one free? She smirked and stood again. Her eyes were alive and I knew she loved this. She placed her hands on my knees and bent at the waist, her face inches from mine, her dark brown hair tumbling around her face.

"Do I have your permission?" She asked.

I played along because I'm twisted like that. If it turned her on, it turned me on, and that was just an inescapable truth for us. "No. I do not give you permission. You are engaged to me. Get undressed and back in bed and let's watch a movie together."

I saw goose bumps on her arms.

"I'm going to go fuck Darryl now," she said, turning to leave, walking to the door.

The moment is forever burned into my brain. She looked so hot and sexy it broke my heart.

\*\*\*

The waiting, as I'm sure you can imagine, was pure psychological warfare. I calculated seven minutes for her to drive to the Hyatt, three minutes to get to the elevator, three more to ride, another two to walk to his room. Within fifteen minutes she's with him inside his room. Does he kiss her at the door? Do they talk first and try to relax?

Fifteen minutes later and I'm pacing our room. After thirty I'm insanely horny and take my dick out and play with it, but I don't let myself orgasm. I don't know what the night has in store for me and I want to be ready.

Forty-five.

Sixty.

After an hour I'm so hot I want to peel off my own skin. I'm sure he's fucking Macy at that very moment. I rationalize I should just go ahead and cum because I'll have time to recover, so I do. The orgasm is so powerful it feels like my head explodes. I'm dizzy and seeing stars.

Thirty more minutes. She's been gone an hour and a half. I know he's fucked her by now. There's no way a guy like Darryl wouldn't have fucked her by now. A stud like him has probably already fucked her twice. I see her spreading her legs. I see her sucking his big black cock. Image after image attacks my mind.

Thirty more minutes. My fiancée has been alone with another man for two hours. My penis is already hard again, proving my theory correct. Big fucking deal.

Ten minutes later the phone rings. I answer. Macy's sweet, musical voice.

"Hi Sweetie. How are you?"

"I'm fine. Going insane actually. How are you?"

She sounds amazing. Within her voice I hear layers of love, excitement, adventure, lust, humor.

"Oh Baby," she lilts. "I am absolutely wonderful. Did you jack off?"

Shit. "Yes."

"I thought you would. Was it good?"

"Yes."

"This is very exciting isn't it Honey? I've climaxed too. Three times in fact. Does that upset you or excite you?"

My heart leaped inside my chest; *Darryl made her cum three times!*

"Both, if I'm honest." I dreaded asking the next question. She answered it before I could.

"Darryl climaxed too, James. Twice already. Would you like to guess where?"

"Inside your pussy?"

"Is that where you'd want him to pump his cum?"

"Yes."

"Are you absolutely sure about that Honey? You would want another man to fill your fiancée with his sperm?"

She was fucking ruthless. I know she was just having fun with it but Jesus, she was ruthless.

"Yes! Where are you?"

28

"I'm in his bed Baby. I'm on top of him. His big black cock is inside my pussy right now holding all that cum inside me like a plug. Do you want to come up and join us or are you happy in our room jerking off and imagining me?"

"I want to join you."

"I was hoping you'd say that my Love. Hyatt. Room nine ninety. See you soon."

She hung up in a hurry but before she did I heard her moan. Since I had masturbated earlier I decided a shower was needed so fifteen minutes later I was dressed and outside hailing a cab. The ride to the Hyatt was six minutes.

I strode through the lobby like I owned it. Jab the button, wait. Doors open, I step in, doors close, jab button number nine, lean back against the mirrored wall and wonder what the fuck I am getting myself into. Doors open and I walk the hall. Nine Ninety is last door on the right. I take a deep breath, slid the card, enter.

One of the black guys from the show just stares at me. Jesus, these guys are huge. Three of them are sitting around the living room; two on the couch, facing the television, one in a chair. It's the one in the chair looking me up and down. He stands with a question in his eyes. The lights are low and the room is mostly illuminated by the television set, which is tuned to Sports Center on ESPN.

"Macy? Darryl?" I ask the black redwood tree in front of me.

From the back of the room I hear Macy say, "He's okay guys, he's with me." Her voice gets louder as she gets closer.

When I finally see her, I'm stunned. All she's wearing are the thigh-high black boots. Her tits are pink and her nipples swollen. Her pussy has a glaze of cum coating the inner lips. The insides of her thighs are streaked with semen. Her hair's a mess. Her face is glowing and her cheeks are flush and her smile stretches from one ear to the other. I swear she is arching her spine a little just to stick out her ass in back and her tits in front. All three guys casually ogle every inch of her fantastic body. She makes no effort to hide her nakedness at all, enjoying their eyes on her flesh. She takes

29

my hand and leads me past these guys to the bedroom at the back.

She enters first and then closes the door behind me. Darryl is spread eagle on the bed, puffing on a joint. He's as big as a dinosaur. It's a king sized bed and he covers more than half of it. His jet black monster cock hangs down on top of his balls and rests on the bed. He acknowledges me with a quick nod of his head.

Macy slithers back up on the bed with him; her legs tangle with his and her head rests on his stomach. She is still smiling at me but the smile has changed; it has an edge to it now, a tease behind her hazel eyes. She reaches down and hefts Darryl's weighty cock like a fire hose, pointing it at me. How thick is Darryl's cock? With her hand wrapped around the base of this beast, there is about a two inch gap between her fingertips and her thumb.

She winks and opens her mouth and stands him straight up and I see what she meant about his balls but she was way off; they're like *my* fists inside a bag, not hers. His balls are truly massive. How much semen do they produce? How much has he already injected into my fiancée?

Her eyes are locked on mine as the plump head of his cock disappears into her mouth. Her cheeks dent as she sucks hard on him. I have no idea what I'm supposed to do here. I see a big chair by the bed so I move to it and sit. Macy's head is bobbing slowly on his shaft. She's in no hurry. She's not trying to make him orgasm. She just loves sucking his big black cock and playing with his heavy balls so she is spending some time doing that. My nuts tightened watching her little pink tongue paint his shaft and head with her saliva. She snakes the tip into the hole at the end of his cock, she sucks one nut into her mouth and rolls it around, then repeats her performance with his other nut. Her ass is turned towards me slightly and I glance down at her bare naked pussy. Some of Darryl's cum is leaking out and down her butt cheek.

Darryl is the King of the World. He lies there, totally relaxed, smoking a joint while one of earth's hottest women worships his cock like a slut. He drops a hand down her back to her ass and slips a thick finger in her pussy. My fiancée moans.

He has grown hard again from Macy's attention. She looks up at him and says something I can't hear and rolls on top of him. Her strong thighs straddle his narrow hips. She reaches under her pussy and stands his big cock straight up again and with her other hand spreads her labia. She rubs his dick back and forth a few times then lowers her hole until it covers his cock-head. He's so big her outer lips stretch to accommodate him. My heart rate is increasing fast. Part of me wants to panic but the rest of me wants to howl with raw lust.

His hard cock is a tower of black, vein-covered meat. Macy's little pink pussy struggles to handle him. The contrast of their skin is sexy and erotic and taboo I want so badly to see that huge dick slide into her tight cunt. I don't have to wait long. Darryl lifts his hips a little and Macy lowers hers a little and inch by slow inch Darryl disappears inside Macy. In less than a minute they start a rhythm of up and down. Macy tosses her head and cries out at the intensity of the pleasure of Darryl's cock.

I watch the two of them together and I have to admit, it's wildly sexy. Macy's hot little female body is the perfect match to his giant male body. A fear takes hold inside me; they look more natural together, as lovers more in-tune with each other, than Macy and I do. I watch as my fiancée loses herself to the sensations of fucking Darryl.

Soon he stands up and moves her to all fours. His huge black cock sticks out from his massive, muscular body like a rhinoceros's horn. It arches up from his hips like a weapon. For a moment I fear for Macy's safety. He bends it down and lines it up and sinks it into her dripping wet pussy and the absolutely satisfied sigh that escapes her throat tells me I needn't have worried. He pulls in all the surrounding skin on every thrust and Macy loves it. In less than five minutes he makes her orgasm faster and harder than I ever have, and as I am soon to discover, that was only the first of many. Now that I am there watching her Macy has the audience she craved. Her excitement skyrockets. She's a bad girl behaving

31

poorly and she loves it. Over the next hour, his huge cock rips one orgasm after another from her.

Eventually I can't take any more. My feelings of inadequacy and worries about suffering by comparison just don't matter anymore. I have to have her. I strip naked and move to her face where she joyfully and greedily sucks my penis into her mouth. I'm rough with her and she really seems to like it, which encourages me to be rougher. Soon he and I are both fucking her like a dirty whore. She totally gets into it and cums screaming several times.

Darryl and I switch ends and he fucks her mouth while I fuck her pussy. Later we switch back and that's where we are when he fills her pussy, yet again, with his hot load and I empty my nuts down her throat. He recovers twenty minutes later but I don't so he moves up between her legs missionary style and fucks her again. Thirty minutes after that she's busy sucking him again and then rides him until she cum once more and he fills her pussy up with more of his sperm. I add mine to his, fucking her from behind while she's laying on her stomach recovering.

By the time Macy and I started getting dressed, we'd been there fucking for hours, she two hours longer than me. She let Darryl keep her black lace panties and I took her back to our motel leaking cum from her pussy. We were both exhausted so neither of us showered. We just stripped and crawled into bed and snuggled and fell asleep.

Sunday morning dawned bright and clear. Macy and I got up and showered and dressed. All morning neither of us mentioned the night before, although Macy bounced around our room with new energy and couldn't stop smiling.

We grabbed a quick bagel as I drove her to the exhibit hall. We were early so I walked her to her booth. All the other girls were already there too, as were the four black guys next door. As Macy and I walked up, all of her girlfriends looked up at us one by one and grinned. I realized the Big Brothas must have talked. In particular, the girls all looked at me and smiled. Fuck. They all knew Darryl had fucked my sweet fiancée. I was about to feel embarrassment when I noticed they weren't

32

actually looking at me with scorn, but something closer to appreciation or admiration.

Then I understood; this was not a typical group of girls. This was a worldly, lusty, cheating harem of bad girls and now Macy had joined their ranks and done it with her man's consent and participation. They were *envious*. Stacey walked up and led Macy away by an elbow while I set our stuff behind the table. I looked at them and saw they were deep in a fast and whispered conversation. Stacey glanced at me a couple times and I saw desire and surprise. Holy shit! Stacey wanted to fuck me! I looked her hot body up and down and let her catch me. A sly smile spread across her pretty face. Macy saw it.

In six fast steps Macy crossed the distance between us and put her face close to mine.

"No," she emphatically stated.

I looked at her questioningly.

"Don't act stupid," she said, lowering her voice. "No. You do not get to have Stacey or any other woman for that matter. This is not about us trying out different partners. This is about me with other men. If this is so you can enjoy other women, forget it."

I held her angry eyes for a heartbeat or two but then relented. Truth is I don't want other women. It was nice that they wanted me and I loved that hot Stacey wanted to jump my bones, but honestly, Macy was all I really wanted.

"Okay my Love," I said, taking her gorgeous face into my hands. "You're right. It's nice to feel wanted but I don't actually want anyone but you."

Her angry face softened instantly. This was not the fight she was expecting.

I continued. "Stacey is pretty but you're my Goddess. You can have all the other men you want. I just want you."

She surprised me with a joyful squeal and then she jumped off the ground and wrapped her legs around my waist. We kissed ardently. When I looked up Stacey had moved away. With Macy's legs wrapped around me like that I remembered her womb was at that moment full of me and Darryl. Fucking hot.

The last day of these conventions is always very relaxed. Everybody has already made their connections or held their meetings or passed out all their business cards. The convention may officially run to five o'clock tonight, but really it will be over by two or three. I tucked away the last of Macy's stuff and kissed her again and told her to text me when things were wrapping up.

I hadn't seen as much of the waterfront as I'd wanted so that's where I headed. The morning passed quickly. For lunch I ate at a little bistro overlooking the bay and I opened my laptop to get some work done. The cute waitress flirted with me so she got a big tip.

About an hour later my phone buzzed with a text from Macy.

"You know, there's something I've always wanted to do..."

I waited for the second part but nothing came. Finally I text her back.

"I'm listening..."

Nothing. No response. I figured she got busy at the booth so I waited thirty minutes before texting her again.

"What baby? What do you want to do?"

Silence. What the hell? I doubted she would be busy with a customer this long. Then it occurred to me perhaps that text wasn't meant for me. I wracked my brain but came up with no conceivable scenario where if it wasn't meant for me I should care about it. It could mean a million different things. I was stuck; I couldn't go to the hall and look in on her unless I wanted to try the janitor trick again, and I didn't. I couldn't text her because clearly, she wasn't answering those. I couldn't call her for the same reason. If I did go to the hall and she wasn't ready to leave I'd have to wait around bored out of my mind.

Finally I sent her another text.

"Okay, I'm confused. Let me know what's going on."

I sat at that bistro overlooking the water for two more hours. I got a lot of work done but my mind was always on Macy.

34

Now I knew it was okay to go by the hall. Even if she wasn't ready to go, the wait would not be a long one. I packed up and drove back to the convention center. The loading dock was wide open as were all the doors to the hall. I walked through and discovered workers already disassembling the various display and tables. Almost all the civilians were already gone. I quickened my pace to Macy's booth.

Everyone was gone. Nobody was here. I walked around backstage and discovered their gym bags and purses were gone too. Where was Macy? I realized I had been holding my breath and let it go. Not knowing what else to do, I went back to the car and drove to the Hyatt.

I admit I was nervous. On the elevator ride up I wondered what my plan was. I no longer had the room key. I would have to knock. What if no one answered the door? What if they answered and told me to fuck off? I was running several possible scenarios through my head when I reached out and knocked on the door. After a minute, I knocked again. The door opened and one of the black guys stood there holding a towel around his waist. I used the same thing I had said the night before.

"Macy? Darryl?"

He walked away from the door with a "Shut it and lock it." spoken over his shoulder. I entered into a cloud of pot. The heavy drapes were drawn so the room was dark. After two steps he dropped his towel. I shut the door and locked it and followed him to the back bedroom.

The first thing I saw as I turned the corner was Stacey, hot, gorgeous, totally nude Stacey, walking towards me, drying her hair with a towel.

When she saw me she smiled and tossed the towel onto the back of a chair, then put her hands on her hips, allowing me an unobstructed view of her glorious body, which I greedily drank in. The tall, naked black man came up behind her and she leaned her body back against his. He offers a roach to her lips and she pulled on it, the cherry glowing bright red in the dim room. He cupped one of her big boobs and rolled her nipple.

35

"You want some?" he asked, like Stacey was his to offer.

I looked her up and down again. God-fucking-damn.

Stacey and I locked eyes and she said, "I would so fuck the shit out of you."

I sighed from down deep. There was nothing to say.

"Have you seen Macy?" I asked.

She stared at me another second or two, probably wondering how the fuck I was able to resist a naked Stacey offering herself to me, which I have to admit I was wondering myself right then, and then she took my hand and walked me across the suite to the master bedroom. She stopped at the door.

"Are you sure about this?" she asked.

Since I had no idea what she was referring to, I nodded.

"Okay then," she concluded. "Best of luck to you. I'm gonna get dressed and go. My husband will be picking me up soon." She opened the door and backed away.

The cloud of pot smoke swirled as the door passed through it. Candles provided a little more light in here but not much. As my eyes adjusted, I heard things before I saw them.

Macy whimpered from pleasure.

A man growled deeply.

Macy gasped as flesh began to slap flesh.

Another, different male voice telling someone to open their mouth.

Macy moaned loudly.

I stepped into the room. On the king-sized bed, Macy, nude, in the center and on her hands and knees. One of the black men, the tallest one, was behind her, pumping his hard cock in and out of her little pussy. Darryl leaned against the headboard with his massive arms spread wide along the top. Macy was between his spread-open legs sucking his cock like she needed his sperm to live. A third black guy stood next to the one fucking her stroking his cock and waiting his turn with her pussy. When I looked down at his hand I was stunned. His dick was bigger than Darryl's.

The guy fucking her pulled his cock out and let his friend step up. The Biggest Dick guy rubbed his huge cock-head around her pussy to wet it and then lined it up and leaned his weight in. Macy cried out around Darryl's dick at the intrusion. He held her hips, not allowing her to get away, and slowly began to working his cock in and out. Macy must have been soaked because soon he was really driving it home and she was going crazy. Her big firm tits jerked back and forth each time his hips crashed into her butt.

I fell back against the wall to watch.

When Darryl climaxed he held her head down and made her swallow all of it. She was still sucking on the head when he took his dick away from her. Tall black guy slipped into Darryl's place and Macy held his cock up and sucked him down.

Biggest Dick guy and Tall guy were not gentlemen. I mentioned earlier that Macy normally would never go for guys like these and that was true. But now she was too far gone, too horny, and too hot for cock.

Biggest Dick held Macy's hips like a vise and fucked her hard. Her abs were tight and the muscles in her back writhed. She was screaming and crying but still egging him on, slamming her hips back at him. When she came all over his huge cock he didn't even slow down. Tall guy was equally rough with her mouth. He kept forcing more and more down her throat every time until she was taking over half his cock on every upward thrust of his hips. She gagged often but would not back away. Her nipples were more erect than I can ever remember seeing them.

The guys said something to each other and they changed positions again. Fuck that guys dick was big. When he waved it in Macy's face her eyes rolled back and she moaned loudly. I swear she almost climaxed.

"You just had this monster *inside* me?" she asked in disbelief.

She dove on his big balls with her tongue, swabbing his nuts.

Tall guy got into position behind her and rested his big black dick between her butt cheeks. He pulled a sheet to wipe the sweat off his face and asked Darryl to grab the bong for him, which Daryl did. Tall guy took a hit and leaned around and placed it in front of Macy, the huge muscles on his back, arm, and thighs all flexing and curling with his movements. She let go of that massive dick long enough to pull from the glass tube as Tall guy lit her up. She held it as long as she could then coughed out a huge cloud of dense smoke.

That was when I realized she didn't even know I was here.

Adrenaline shot through my veins. That thought gave me such a rush! This was one hundred percent real! She was not up on a stage showing off for me this time. She was doing all this just for her. She was a purely sexual creature with only the pursuit of pleasure in mind. She had forgotten all about me and I loved it!

I slowly sat on a foot-stool and made myself small. To the guys I was already invisible. If I wanted to join in they'd say sure, have some, but they weren't going to invite me. They were too busy with my Macy themselves. How long had they already been at it? How long had these studs been fucking my hot little fiancée? I thought back to that very first text telling me about something she's always wanted to do. Did it start then? Did Shane cut them all loose early? That was about one o'clock this afternoon. They could have all been at this for over two hours already. So hot!

Tall guy grabbed each of Macy's round butt cheeks. He pulled them up and apart, splitting her ass and obscenely exposing her little pussy. He pulled his hips back and the head of his dick mashed her pussy lips, resting there for the moment. He eased forward and his cock disappeared inside her. She hung her head and just whimpered as he fucked her. He lifted his pelvis and really started slamming it deep. His fat black balls smash her clit over and over. She couldn't take very much of that before she came hard. Before too long he sped up and announced to all of us it was coming. When his orgasm hit he pushed his cock as deep as he could and pumped his seed into her. After the last drop was inside, he left the bed and sat on the love-seat and dropped his head back like he was exhausted.

Macy was wiped out. She kept her ass and pussy up in the air but I saw her legs trembling. She slowly turned her attention to that huge dick in her face and leisurely began to suck the head and lick the shaft and balls.

The door opened and Dereck, the guy that had been with Stacey, entered the room naked and shut the door. He looked right at Macy's pussy, on display in open invitation. He looked at Darryl and raised his eyebrows, asking for permission. He looked at Darryl. Not me, Macy's fiancée. He had to check with Darryl to make sure it was okay if he fucked Macy. Darryl gave him permission with a little wave of his hand and Dereck wasted no time.

"Ron," he said to Biggest Dick man. "Give me her mouth. I've wanted her to suck my dick from the moment I saw her."

Macy laughed and wiped the back of her hand across her mouth.

"I've wanted to suck your dick from the moment I saw you, too."

Ron moved out of the way and let Dereck take his place. Macy ran her fingers over his cock and balls.

"You're cute," she said. "Stacey snagged you for herself before I could."

"Ha! I wanted you too but Darryl said no, you belonged to him. Darryl so rarely stakes a claim that when he does, we all give Darryl what he wants."

Macy turned to face Darryl. If I would have moved she would have spotted me so I remained motionless.

"Baby," she said to Darryl. "Is that true? Do I belong to you?"

Darryl nodded his head slowly and confidently. A small grin spread his lips.

"But I share," he rumbled.

Ron had moved around behind her and his huge black dick pointed right at her cunt. He smacked her ass bringing a yelp from Macy and then pulled her and pushed her until he had her right where he wanted her. He again rubbed his massive cock-head around her labia to wet it and then split her open and began feeding it to her pussy. His large, rock-hard ass-muscles flexed and tightened as he pushed it in.

"Oh my GOD!" Macy yelled. She dropped her head to the blanket for the moment forgetting all about Dereck. Ron kept steady pressure, slowly inching his monster back inside my girl. I wondered how much semen she already carried. I'm sure all of them had fucked her at least once.

Ron's cock was working magic on Macy. With each new inch she was tossing her head and moaning. I'd never seen her like this. Dereck was getting into it too. His dick stood like a flagpole in front of Macy's face. Ron withdrew some and pushed it back in, then again only a little farther.

Dereck smiled and said, "We should have drug Stacey in here with you and then all four of us had some fun at the same time."

Macy looked up at him.

"I don't like sex with girls. I love being fucked by men. I love dick."

"That's cool," he replied. "So then here, suck this dick." Macy dropped her open mouth on his cock-head, enveloping and sucking. He moved her hair so he could watch his inches pumping in and out of her mouth. She could only take less than half but he seemed content with that.

Ron had given her enough time to adjust to his size. His shaft was slick with her juices and while he still had to force the last few inches to get them inside her, he wasn't hurting her. He held her hips lightly and started fucking her pussy with long, deep strokes. Macy tried to concentrate on the blowjob she was giving but Ron's dick made it just about impossible for her. She was gasping and groaning with every breath.

All three of them slowly got serious. Soon Macy was making animal sounds as Ron worked her tight pussy. Even in the dark I saw how her lips were stretched wide to accept him. They began to move in-time with each other, the guys fucking the hot babe, the hot babe loving the big, hard cocks being used on her.

Macy held on to Dereck's thighs as she started to cum again, and it was a powerful one. Ron kept his rhythm strong

40

and steady and just let Macy orgasm all over him. He waited for her to come down before he increased his speed and depth. She rested her head on Dereck's stomach. I'd never heard her make sounds like she was making right now.

"I'm gonna fill this cunt to over-flowing. Best piece of ass I've ever had! Goddamn your pussy is tight. Here it comes. Take it all. Holy shiiiiit!"

Ron dumped an ocean of cum inside Macy. I couldn't see exactly how much but he just kept grunting and groaning and jerking his hips. When he finally withdrew his semi-erect spear, it was covered with pearly white fluid. He moved to the edge of the bed and let his phallus hang down and drip on the floor.

"Jamal," he said to the Tall Guy on the love-seat. "Get your ass back over here."

Jamal nodded a few times and stood. Darryl stood too.

"This sexy bitch," he said. "Needs all three of us at the same time. Ron, you're out. Your dick is too big." All four of them laughed and I heard Macy mumble "Thank God."

Darryl lay on his back and Macy straddled him. He started to guide his big black dick into her cunt but she stopped him and said, "Allow me." Dereck stood up right where he was and steered his cock back into Macy's mouth. Jamal waited his turn, allowing all of them to get positioned, then stepped up to Macy's ass and pushed her down onto Darryl's chest.

Macy was understandably worried at first but Darryl held her face in his huge hands and muttered sweet things and kissed her eyelids. Macy relaxed and returned to sucking Dereck's cock and Darryl distracted her by working her nipples hanging in his face and Jamal gradually eased his hard dick-head past her sphincter and an inch up her ass. Macy moaned like she'd been shot so Jamal pulled back a bit and then pushed three inches deep. Macy took her mouth off Dereck's dick long enough to gasp, "Oh my God!" and then slide that cock back in her mouth.

All three men began to fuck her. I'll never forget that sight as long as I live. Macy arched her back to help the guys fuck her ass and pussy and her big tits stuck out in front. Her

41

butt muscles worked her hips and she forced as much of Dereck's cock down her throat as she could get. She gagged often but that didn't stop her. She never did take the whole thing, but she came close. Dereck surprised me by being the first to cum, pumping a big load of semen into her tummy and the last few jets onto her waiting tongue, then staggering away to a chair near me. Macy laughed with delight at how she had wrecked him.

With him out of the picture the guys were able to fuck Macy deeper and harder. With his dick out of her mouth her moans and groans of mind-bending pleasure filled the room. The neighbors probably thought we were killing someone with hammers. For reasons unknown to me, watching this part got to me more than any other time and my dick grew.

Jamal and Darryl used Macy's holes, driving their massive ebony dicks as far into her as they could get them. Macy came again but this one was so powerful it left her weak and limp. The guys just kept fucking her rag-doll body. Something about being used like this must have touched something really deep within her because after just a few minutes Macy came again even harder than the last one, surprising everyone including herself. She burst into tears and was sobbing as both men continued to fuck her.

Jamal climaxed next, pumping his black baby seed deep into her bowels. He stayed inside her a while as he softened and eventually was squeezed out by her tight ass. He went back to his place on the love-seat, dropping heavily into the cushions.

Darryl worked his fat fingers into Macy's thick hair. He pulled her face down to his and slowed the tempo of his upwards thrusts. Her sobs had abated but tears still streaked her face. He delicately moved a few strands of hair off her face and behind her ears.

"You love it, don't you Baby-girl?"

Macy sniffed and slowly nodded her head.

"You have feelings for me and my boys don't you?"

Again Macy nodded a yes. His hips were rising and falling very gradually now, his cock pumping in and out in a slow, sensuous way.

"That's good Macy. We all have feelings for you too. You are something special."

Bullshit or not his words were having an effect on her. She smiled and sniffed hard and then laughed a little. He laughed too.

"I always form an attachment," she croaked. "I hate it. Why can't I just fuck and be fucked? My pussy is connected to my heart. I always fall in love with whoever is fucking me."

Darryl laughed out loud.

"Because you're sweet and true and the world hasn't soiled you yet. Do you love your man? What's his name, James?"

Macy nodded enthusiastically and without hesitation and I breathed a sigh of relief.

"Then just give it a few days. Your emotions for me and my guys will fade. We went through a lot together. We connected to you too. We'll always have that special bond and next time we're in Vegas, you can count on all of us looking you up."

It was Macy's turn to laugh.

"You'd better," she said.

Darryl pulled her tight against his chest and pushed it all the way in and held it buried balls deep. Macy gasped loudly. Then he withdrew all but the head and did it again, holding it longer this time. Then he did it again, holding it deep up inside her even longer.

Macy groaned. "Oh my God Darryl, I love being fucked by you. I love your body. I love your big black cock." Darryl grunted and fucked up into her faster. She wrapped her arms around the back of his head and mashed her hard young tits against his huge chest.

"There's something I've wanted to ask you," Darryl growled. "Are you on birth control?"

"No!" Macy exclaimed.

Darryl chuckled. "I like that," he said. "There are a lot of black baby seeds in your womb right now. How you feel about that?"

"I love it," Macy grunted between thrusts. "I'm not ready for a baby. I'm way too young. But all that sperm inside me is

43

like proof, proof I really did it, I really went all the way. I get so hot knowing it's in there."

My penis was hard as diamond.

"Me too. It's the ultimate. I want to give you some more. Swear you'll fuck me again when I come to Vegas next month."

"Oh my God yes, of course; I swear it. Darryl, you can fuck me whenever you want. I'll handle James. I'll make him understand."

Darryl rolled her onto her back and moved between her wide open legs and really started hammering her with his cock. Macy's head rolled side to side as her hips unconsciously rose to meet his on every thrust. I'm sure her pussy was milking his giant cock just like it does mine, but no doubt it felt way better for him.

"Oh my fucking God!" Macy gasped, surprised. "I don't believe it!"

Before she was ready yet another orgasm slammed into her and she screamed and pulled up the sheets. Her whole body rose and fell like she was being electrocuted and she screamed again and arched her back hard. Darryl drew a huge breath and bore down on her and then he too was yelling, telling her to take every drop. His semen started to push out around his shaft and drip down her ass. He came a long time before collapsing his giant body on top of hers. She almost disappeared. His weight was too much and he quickly rolled to her side, his long, black python slithering out of her pussy and flopping against his leg. They both lay there gasping for breath.

After a while he leaned in and kissed her forehead and then rose and left the bed. He signaled to his troops and they all left the room together, closing the door behind them.

Macy stared at the ceiling for a long time. I was a statue. I would have paid a million dollars to know what she was thinking at that moment. She was a well-fucked mess. I memorized every square inch of her young, tight flesh. What a Goddess. She seemed to ponder something and reached a finger down to her pussy. She pushed it inside then brought it up to examine it. Her finger was shiny even in the dark and a

44

drop of cum hung from the tip. She swirled the drop around her thumb and fingertips.

She thought of something and giggled and reached for her cell phone on the far nightstand. I suspected she was about to text or call me so while her back was turned I cautiously pulled out my phone and had it ready. First she read through all the texts I had sent. Then she lay back down and opened her legs wider and pushed a few buttons, then reached down and snapped a picture of her thoroughly fucked cunt. She checked to make sure she liked it and added text and hit send.

When my phone chimed and lit up just across the room, she jumped, her head snapped to the side and she squinted.

"Holy fucking Christ!" she yelled. "How long have you been there? What the fuck?" She slowly closed her legs.

I raised a finger and muttered "I told you I have Ninja powers. Hold on, got a text."

The picture was raw and nasty and erotic and I loved it. Sweet Macy's pussy lips were battered and puffy and streaked and glazed with cum. A stream of sperm leaked from her hole and disappeared between her ass cheeks. The text read, "And now I've done it. Sorry I didn't wait for you, but I just couldn't." It was glorious.

I tucked my phone into my shirt pocket. Macy's face was a mask of dismay and fear. I had seen her lose control and give herself completely to another. I had witnessed her total surrender to another man, to other men, and she had never intended that to happen. She was sure she had gone too far. Her lip trembled. Tears seemed imminent.

I understood. This had been something outside our game. This had been something just for her. This was something dark and dangerous and Macy was certain nobody would understand. She'd probably had these erotic thoughts as long as she's been thinking about sex but growing up in that all-white town left her no place to put them and no one to talking about them with. By the time she met me she'd put so much energy into burying them they were no longer accessible to her, not directly.

45

But then this weekend happened and circumstances made the unthinkable possible, even easy. She couldn't stop herself. Her desire swelled up and compelled her and rather than risk asking me and being told no, she just took what she wanted, what she desperately wanted. This all would have worked if only I hadn't seen her tender submission.

I understood, but that didn't make it okay. Technically, Macy had just cheated on me, and done it with four black guys, and developed feelings for at least a few and possibly all of them. I walked over and stood looking down on her. She tried pulling the sheets and blankets to cover her but since most of them had gotten pushed off onto the floor, that didn't work too well. Fuck me she was beautiful.

So what was my move? The real truth was I *liked* that she cheated on me. My big fear with revealing that truth was I basically would be giving her permission to do whomever she wanted, whenever she wanted, and the option of telling me or not rested with her, and I'm sorry, but relationships have to have *some* boundaries.

So what was my move?

Macy made it for me.

Taking my lack of screaming and anger as an indication of how I was really feeling, she'd regained her composure while I was running all these thoughts through my head. On her knees now at the edge of the bed she pulled down my zipper and unbuckled my belt. She worked my pants down to my knees. Her eyes weren't entirely confident. She was playing a hunch. She fell onto her back and opened her legs right at me.

"Mad?" she asked, coy.

"Some. A little. You know technically you cheated on me."

She waved a hand in the air. "Who cares? I'll never leave you. I'll always love you."

So she was taking the 'best defense is a good offense' route.

"Besides," she continued. "Not only did I kind of involve you, I totally would have told you everything afterwards, and that would have made us both so hot we'd fuck about it."

46

She stretched her body like a cat, rolling her hips, causing her breasts to slide first to one side then to the other. She closed her legs and rolled onto her stomach, then lifted her ass just a little. Her cum-filled diamond was aimed right at me. My penis lifted a little.

"Do you want to eat my pussy? You're staring right at it."

"No, not at the moment."

"Why not Lover?"

"Because it's full of cum."

She practically purred. "God! It gets me so hot to hear you say that. It is, isn't it? I fucked all of them Baby. I'm so dirty. I'm such a slut. You sure you want to marry me? You know you won't be able to control me, right? You know I'm sure to get myself into more trouble, with or without your permission."

She rose up on her knees and cupped both of her big tits. A sly smile played across her lips. She was perfect. I couldn't take my eyes off of her.

"You're perfect," I said. I couldn't help it. It just came out.

Her eyes lit up. She had me now.

"But look at me Honey, I'm a slutty mess."

I did. She was.

"Jack off for me James. Will you do it? I want to feel your eyes all over me, looking like this. I want to see you lusting after your naughty fiancée."

She lay back down and played with her tits. She slipped a finger down to feel the glut of semen in her pussy again. I reached for my dick.

It took me hardly any time at all. Fuck she's so hot. She twisted and turned and showed me every dirty thing she had done. She talked about the two hours before I got there and how she and Stacey had fucked Darryl and Dereck in the same room at the same time and how hot it was watching Stacey get fucked. When she reminded me that I would never get to fuck Stacey, I came.

***

47

We had to leave the room to retrieve Macy's clothes but she didn't care. Around these guys she was shameless. Darryl swatted her bare ass as she walked past and for a second I thought things were about to heat up again but they didn't. We all had other places we needed to be.

Our flight out left Monday morning so as is our usual custom, we had the last night after a show all to ourselves. Once the weed and adrenaline wore off, Macy commented a few times how sore she was. I was dying to fuck her but had to wait. We stopped by Shane's room and Macy got paid and discovered Shane had done so well everyone got a bonus.

By Monday night we were back in our home, unpacked, showered, and lying in bed. We'd been talking about landscaping changes to the front yard and conversation had died down and we were both just musing on our own thoughts. It was a very comfortable silence.

"I need to trust your love." Macy stated, staring up at the stucco ceiling.

I looked at her and told her to continue.

"I always go too far. Always. Sex gets a hold on me and I always cross the line. But then I get really scared that you're going to change your mind and decide you don't love me after all. Like, now that I've shown you what a true whore I am you won't want me."

She pulled her eyes away from the ceiling and fixed them on me.

"But you always do. In fact I think you love me more. I'm a very lucky girl."

"I do love you more, after, but I'm the lucky one. You could be with any man you want and you pick me. I need to trust your love too."

We both silently pondered for a moment.

"Mace, Baby," I said. "It scares me to tell you this but I love that you always go too far. I feel by admitting that I'm handing over all my power in this relationship and giving you permission to walk all over me. I really hope you don't. But I love how much you love sex. I love that you get carried away

48

by it. I want to free you and your imagination, not shut you down because of my fears and insecurities."

"Oh my God Honey! That has to be the sweetest thing you have ever said to me! Jesus! I'm all tingly. James, I promise you can trust me too."

We pulled each other closer and snuggled. After more comfortable silence she mumbled, "I think about sex all the time now Baby."

"Good," I said and meant it.

"I'm too sore to do anything about it but I'm horny. I'm warm all over. I'm lying here next to my fiancé with a womb full of semen and almost none of it is his. It turns me on so much. I feel so naughty. We're just hanging out not doing anything about it and it's driving me crazy. The clock is ticking. I don't want to get pregnant but the idea that I could any second makes me horny as fuck. My womanhood is so powerfully in the moment."

My penis stirred and filled some. She felt it.

"I see it has the same effect on you?"

"God yes. I have no idea why and to tell the truth I'm tired of thinking about it and trying to figure myself out. From now on if I like it, I like it. If it makes me horny, it, makes me horny."

"I like that plan. Count me in."

Now all I could think about was those guys fucking my fiancée and all the cum they pumped into her. I'm such a pervert. The need to fuck her was growing inside me but there was nothing I could do; her mouth, her pussy, even her ass was too sore and tender. Within a few minutes I was rock hard and pressed against her hip. She reached down and wrapped her fingers around me and gave my dick a hard squeeze.

"You must be dying," she teased.

"You have no idea. A hand just won't do it for me. Mine or yours."

"Poor Baby," she said, and her voice carried a giggle in it. "Just be patient. I'm sure I'll recover fast. I'm guessing you won't have to wait longer than two or three days."

"What? Why so long? I bet if Darryl walked into the room right now you wouldn't tell him no."

"That's different, Honey. Of course I wouldn't."

I couldn't tell if she was serious or still just fucking with me.

"If Darryl walked into the room right now you'd fuck him?"

"Yes."

"You'd suck his dick?"

"Yes. I'd try to distract him away from my tender ass but if he insisted, I'd give him that too."

I was dumbfounded. I now understood she was serious. What the fuck?

She saw my hurt and confused face and explained.

"Darryl is a big, black, conquering stud. How many more times will I ever see him? Maybe never. I would not pass up the opportunity. You and I are committed to each other for the rest of our lives. If Darryl walked in and wanted me, I just couldn't tell him no. I don't have that option with him, and if he was naked or pulled his cock out where I could see it, I know I couldn't resist. You can wait because we'll always have tomorrow to do it."

I have to admit, it stung.

"What if Dereck walked in?"

"Yes, same thing. Any one of those four guys Baby. Stop looking at it like a man. I'm not a prize to be won. They aren't winning because they would get to fuck me. It's about sex, silly."

"What about that older guy from the Jacuzzi?"

She thought for a moment.

"Ha! No. He's not hot enough and his dick wasn't big enough. He was bigger than you, which I liked, but not big enough to make me act stupid. I'm such a slut. But any one of those black guys would."

She held my face in her hands. "Sweetie, you didn't even ask about Ron. I would do *anything* Ron told me to do. I don't think you realize how many times that man made me orgasm. I was climaxing in-between my climaxes when he was inside me. Jesus! That cock is ridiculous. My pussy was *completely* full. The base of his dick rubbed against my clit at

50

the same time his head reached up past my cervix and nudged the end of my womb. He was *amazing...*"

The anguish she was causing me also fueled my lust. I couldn't take it anymore and started stroking my dick, which I was not at all interested in. I wanted Macy, not my own hand! It hurt knowing that other men walked the earth at that moment that she would fuck right now but that I wasn't one of them. I didn't fully understand her explanation but I got a nagging suspicion what she said actually made sense and some emotional immaturity on my part kept me from getting it. This whole event was a complex mess of thoughts and emotions. I knew some things would only be determined with time. One thing that time would not change was my love and devotion to her. There had been many difficult moments this weekend but I felt closer and more in love with her now than I did just a few days ago. Crazy.

Frustrated and filled with angst, I let go of my dick. It bobbed in the open air, red, angry, rock-hard. Macy saw it and giggled.

"When you can finally have me again, I'm afraid you're going to fuck me to death."

She had a point.

# Afterword

In the weeks that followed something Macy had said kept nagging me: "*Not big enough to make me act stupid.*"

Macy had indirectly warned me what a big dick could do to her and what I should expect if one came around.

Three months later, one did. Not Darryl or even Dereck, but Ron, the longest and thickest of all four of them. He had gotten Macy's number from Darryl and sent her a text. He was in Vegas and would she like to meet for a drink or dinner?

It was Friday night and we were eating burgers and fries at a popular greasy-spoon when the message came in. Macy read it and put her phone back in her purse and went on with our conversation. It was two hours later on our drive home when she finally told me what the text had said. I asked her why she had waited so long to share it with me she said she'd wanted to think about it first.

I was nervous and apprehension gripped my guts. I wondered if this was all still such a great idea. "That's not cool Honey." I said. "You shouldn't leave me out like that."

She smiled weakly.

"So now you've thought about it," I continued. "Please share what you are thinking. I'd like to have some input before you answer him, if you even answer him."

"I already answered him. I responded to him while I was in the restroom back at the restaurant."

My jaw dropped.

"What did you say?" The look in her eye was part mischief, part worry, and part excitement. She drew a deep breath before answering me.

"I gave him our address. He's most likely already there, waiting for us to get home. Are you mad?"

I was. This was supposed to be *our* game, not just something she got to do. I wanted to be angrier but that voice inside my head that finds these moments so incredibly erotic was also making itself heard. A battle raged inside me.

"Why our address Honey? Why would you tell him where we lived? We don't really even know him or any of those guys."

"No, we don't, but that just adds to the excitement in my opinion. I told him because I thought it would be hot to get fucked by him in our bed. Don't you think so Sweetie? Imagine what memories that would create; he used that pillow to prop up my hips or right there is where I held onto the headboard as he pounded me. I think it's so fucking hot I can barely stand it. Just picture what it will do to our sex life Baby. We will never look at our bedroom in the same way again. Ever."

I pictured what she was saying and she was right, but I still felt a little left out of the whole process. She had just

52

invited him over to fuck her without even checking with me. I felt like I needed to reassert myself.

"I have to say, I'm shocked you are going for egotistical muscle-bound guys like this. That has never been your style. What changed?"

"Everything, Sweetie. Once I felt a big cock fucking me I realized how much I'd been lying to myself, playing the role assigned to me. Fuck that. Sex is awesome!"

As I was considering what I would say we turned the corner and the headlights illuminated Ron, wearing tight jeans and a white T-shirt, leaning against his rental car. As soon as I pulled into our driveway Macy was out the door, bouncing across our lawn in her little frilly dress and launching herself into a huge hug, her legs wrapped around his waist and her arms around his neck. I glanced around to see if any neighbors were out and thankfully none were. Macy kissed Ron on the mouth and I hurried to open our front door and get them both inside.

By the time I drew the curtains and lowered the lights I discovered a trail of clothing led to our bedroom. Macy already had the head of his huge black dick in her mouth and her cheeks dented as she sucked hard on him.

Ron stayed that night and the next and the next. He would leave during the day to meet up with his friends, gamble and party, but each night he returned to our home and fucked Macy until sunrise. At first I joined in, adding my cum to his as soon as he pulled out, but after a few orgasms I was spent.

Ron was a machine. I held her and kissed her while Ron fucked her. Sometimes she'd want my soft penis in her mouth while Ron was between her lips. By Saturday night it was just the two of them. Ron got to our place well after two in the morning and woke us up. He smelled of smoke and alcohol but Macy didn't care. She was stroking his dick through his pants before he got his shirt off. I got out of bed and sat nearby, watching and stroking my semi-erect penis, burning every detail of sweet, young Macy giving her perfect body to this conquering demigod.

She could not resist his cock. Tired and tender, she still easily spread her legs or opened her mouth any time he wanted her. Honestly, he fucked her like he was trying to knock-up the hot white chick. He wasn't as smart or as interesting as Darryl but Macy could not have cared less. She was a slave to her senses while he was here and all she wanted was more of him. I knew his plane left very early Monday morning and our minutes together were winding down and I felt disappointment mixed in with a little relief. Macy would probably need to sleep for three straight days to recover, which meant all that time Ron's sperm would be inside her and mine would not. The truth drove me crazy but also turned me on.

The next morning I drove to work after dropping Ron off at the airport. I was beginning to understand the new truth of my relationship with Macy. Weeks ago she had asked me if I would be okay with it and I had agreed. She was not waiting for me to change my mind. My fiancée's appetite for hot men and big, hard cocks could not be ignored or suppressed. I needed to accept there would always be some element of this in our relationship now. If I was going to marry her I'd better be ready accept this about her, and help her attain it. Could I do it?

I thought back to last night; Macy's strong white legs wrapped tightly around Ron's jet-black muscular torso. Her little hands gripped his ass tightly, pulling his big cock down and in as he pounded her. Moans of intense pleasure flowed freely from Macy's throat. I heard my fiancée orgasm yet again on another man's cock.

My penis stirred inside my pants. Ron was on a plane and Macy was home in bed, leaking his cum into our sheets. Am I able to accept this part of Macy?

Oh hell yes. I was already looking forward to our next adventure.

End.

**Visit my blog;** MyEroticBunny.tumblr.com


**Get a FREE Cuckold/Vixen Story!**
**Join My Mailing List**
http://eepurl.com/cTvA7P

Macy and James are onto their next adventure. Some time has passed since their first escapade (Young Love: Macy dates three) and Macy finds herself attracted to a group of men she's never before considered. James can only hold on as Macy's taboo lust takes off again, dragging both on an unexpected odyssey full of lusty sex and angst filled voyeurism.

Author Matthew Lee started the Hotwife lifestyle with his first girlfriend at age sixteen. Virtually every relationship he had from then to now has had some form of sharing included. The books you read here are based on a lifetime of Matthew's sexual experiences.

ISBN 9781973175575

9781973175575